W9-BMM-941

Fun
in the Sun

Editor: Jill Kalz
Page Production: Tracy Kaehler
Creative Director: Keith Griffin
Editorial Director: Carol Jones

First American edition published in 2006 by
Picture Window Books
5115 Excelsior Boulevard
Suite 232
Minneapolis, MN 55416
877-845-8392
www.picturewindowbooks.com

First published in Australia by
Ice Water Press
An imprint of @Source Pty Limited
Unit 3, Level 1, 114 Old Pittwater Road
Brookvale NSW 2100 Australia
Ph: 61 2 9939 8222; Fax: 61 2 99398666
Email: sales@sourceoz.com

Copyright © 2004 by Ice Water Press

Printed in the United States of America.

Library of Congress Cataloging-in-Publication Data
Scott, Janine.
Fun in the sun / by Janine Scott ; illustrated by Ian Forss.
p. cm. — (Farmer Claude and Farmer Maude)
Summary: Tired from too much bad weather, Farmer Claude, Farmer Maude,
and their farm animals go to the beach, where they have time for a bit of fun
before the rain catches up with them.
ISBN 1-4048-1697-6 (hardcover)
[1. Beaches—Fiction. 2. Rain and rainfall—Fiction. 3. Farmers—Fiction. 4. Domestic
animals—Fiction. 5. Stories in rhyme.] I. Forss, Ian, ill. II. Scott, Janine. Farmer
Claude and Farmer Maude. III. Title. IV. Series.
PZ8.3.S4275Fun 2005
[E]—dc22   2005029440

Farmer Claude and Farmer Maude

Fun
in the Sun

by Janine Scott ~ illustrated by Ian Forss

PICTURE WINDOW BOOKS
Minneapolis, Minnesota

Farmer Claude and Farmer Maude
looked at the clouds and sighed,
"For 80 days and 80 nights,
the sky has wept and cried."

They were sick of the rain.
They were sick of the hail.
They were sick of the storms.
They were sick of the gales.

"Where is the sun?" they wailed.

"What should we do?"
cried Farmer Claude.

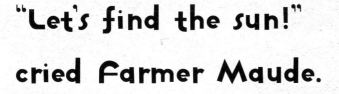

"Let's find the sun!"
cried Farmer Maude.

A cloud is a mass of water drops or ice that floats high in the sky.

7

So Farmer Claude and Farmer Maude
went to find the sun.

The dog, the goat, the rooster, and the pig came along for the sun and the fun.

They drove up the hills

and down the hills,

on highways and byways and trails.

They drove through the city

and then through the town,

through tunnels and bridges with rails.

Then Farmer Claude and Farmer Maude parked near the beach ahead.

"The surf, the sand, the shells, and the sun will be so much fun," they said.

Seventy percent of Earth is covered by salty ocean water.

Farmer Claude and Farmer Maude
walked east in the afternoon.
They built a sand castle down by the sea
and swam in the blue lagoon.

A lagoon is a shallow body of salt water that is separated from the sea by sandbars or coral reefs.

The dog, the goat, the rooster, and the pig
walked west, feeling happy and warm.
But something followed them all the way—
a thunderous, black rainstorm!

Unlike people, pigs cannot sweat when they are hot. They must roll in the mud to stay cool.

17

The shivering animals looked at the sky.
"Where is the sun?" they wailed.
The clouds grew blacker over their heads.
It started to rain, then it hailed.

When it hails, balls of ice fall from the sky.

The dog, the goat, the rooster, and the pig
ran back to the blue lagoon.
But something followed them all the way—
a miserable, wet monsoon!

A monsoon is a very strong wind that usually brings a lot of rain.

The poor, wet animals got back on the truck.
"Oh, where was the sun?" they sighed.
Sand was sticking to their hooves and paws,
and they couldn't get dry, though they tried.

Farmer Claude and Farmer Maude
got into the front of the truck.
"Now that was a day that we'll never forget.
We've really had wonderful luck!"

Farmer Claude and Farmer Maude
looked back at the beach and smiled.
"There was sand, there was sea,
there was plenty of sun,
and the weather was nice and mild."

The dog, the goat, the rooster, and the pig
looked back at the beach with alarm.
"There was sand, there was sea,
but where was the sun?
We should have stayed back on the farm!"

1. How long had it been raining on Farmer Claude and Farmer Maude's farm?

2. Who went along with Farmer Claude and Farmer Maude for some sun and fun?

3. What did Farmer Claude and Farmer Maude do at the beach?

4. What followed the animals when they walked west?

5. What followed the animals when they ran back to the blue lagoon?

6. At the end of the story, where did the animals wish they had stayed?

Rooster's Recap

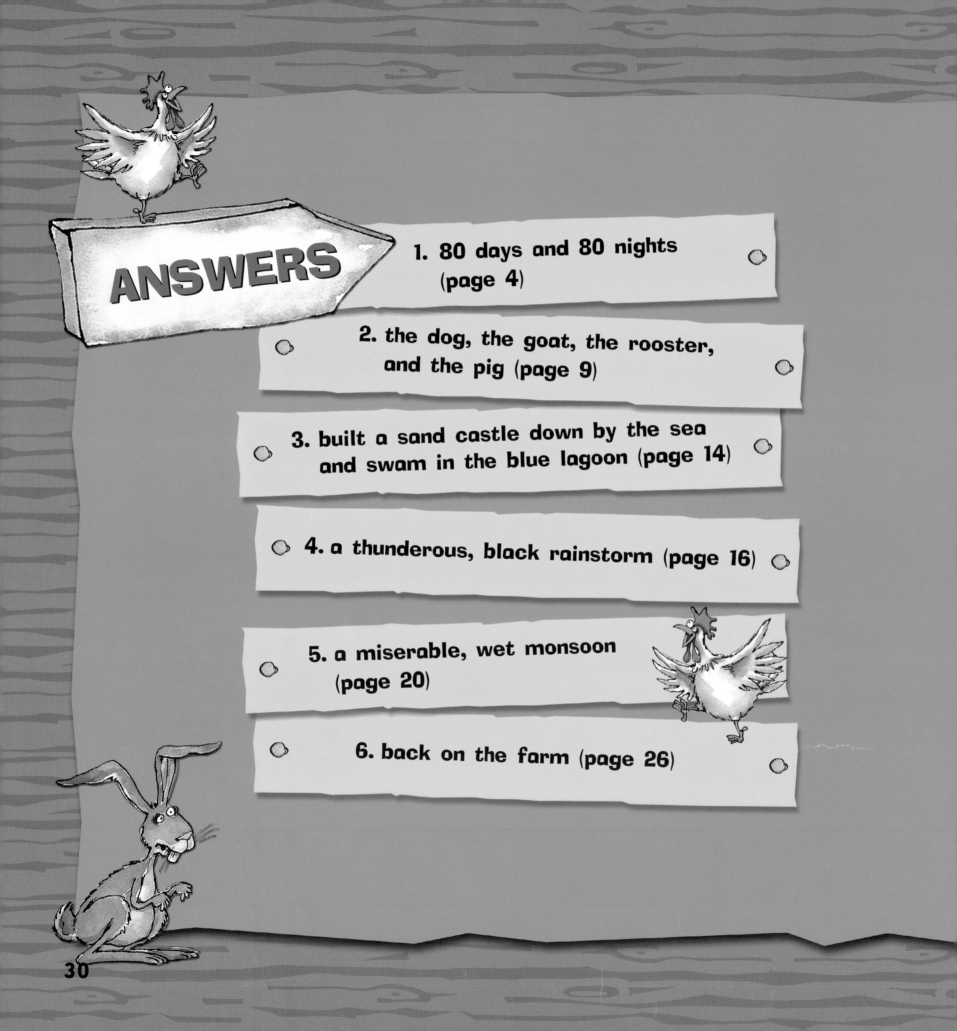

ANSWERS

1. 80 days and 80 nights (page 4)

2. the dog, the goat, the rooster, and the pig (page 9)

3. built a sand castle down by the sea and swam in the blue lagoon (page 14)

4. a thunderous, black rainstorm (page 16)

5. a miserable, wet monsoon (page 20)

6. back on the farm (page 26)

To Learn More

On the Web

FactHound offers a safe, fun way to find Internet sites related to this book. All of the sites on FactHound have been researched by our staff.

1. Visit www.facthound.com
2. Type in this special code for age-appropriate sites: 1404816976
3. Click on the FETCH IT button.

Your trusty FactHound will fetch the best sites for you!

At the Library

Cronin, Doreen. *Click, Clack, Moo: Cows That Type*.
   New York: Simon and Schuster, 2000.

DK Publishing. *Farm Animals*. New York:
   DK Publishing, 2004.

Murphy, Andy. *Out and About at the Dairy Farm*.
   Minneapolis: Picture Window Books, 2004.

Spurr, Elizabeth. *Farm Life*. New York:
   Holiday House, 2003.

READY FOR MORE ADVENTURES?

Charming and funny, Farmer Claude and Farmer Maude are anything but boring. Full of great ideas and in love with adventure, these odd farmers know how to have a good time wherever they are!

Farmer Claude

Farmer Maude

Pig

Goat

Rooster

Dog

What a group of unlucky characters! Storm clouds follow them, rain soaks their beds, and the farmers wake them at the crack of dawn. But the animals make it through together—and even share a smile or two.

Look for All of the Books in the Farmer Claude and Farmer Maude Series: